A WOLF OF MY OWN

STORY BY JAN WAHL

PICTURES BY
LILLIAN HOBAN

The Macmillan Company, New York

Collier-Macmillan Limited, London

For
Heller
and
for
Glory
and
for
you

My birthday.

My birthday.

My birthday!

A striped box with holes.

I hope it's a wolf.

Oh, a little puppy.

Hello.

First you need some water.

Drink up, it's my birthday.

I'll call you Fred.

If you were Fred the wolf child

I would be your wolf friend.

Together we would race across the prairie,

feeling the wind in our fur.

We would find a wolf cave, together,

to take our furry naps in.

Fred, it would be just you and me,

howling at the moon together,

scaring the owls.

We would find the valley of the twisting river,

but we would not swim in the river.

Young wolves do not swim.

Fred, if I caught an antelope

I would share it with you.

I would sing you a wolf song without any words,

when it rained and we crouched under bushes.

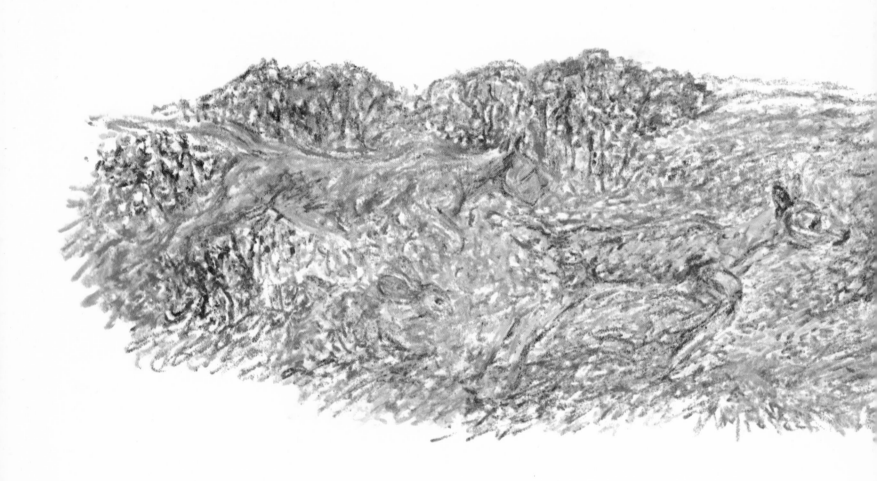

The other animals would run like fire

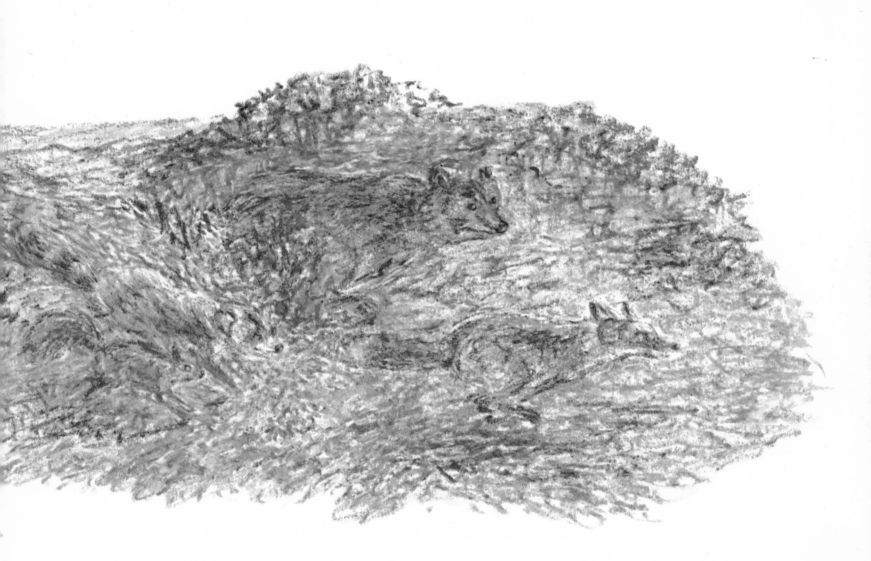

when we approached them.

Campers would hide in their flimsy tents

when we walked through their camps.

We would roll in the grass

this way and that.

And only when the woods

grew cold and dark

would we come home.

It is hard for wolves to climb stairs.

So now I will carry you.

I can walk on my hind feet.

It is time to be in our wolf nest.

Goodnight, wolf brother.

Date Due

FEB 11 70	FACULTY	SEP 18			
SE 2 8 '70	MY 15 75				
JA 31 '72	AG 1 75				
OCT 30 72	MY 29 '76				
DEC 15 72	DEC 9 '77				
SE 29 '73	NOV 29 '79				
SE 30 73	JUL 30 1988				
	OCT. 04 1994				
FE 4 '74					
MR 7 '74	DEC 20 1999				